Acting Edition

the ripple, the wave that carried me home

by Christina Anderson

FOR PRODUCTION INQUIRIES

UNITED STATES AND CANADA
info@concordtheatricals.com
1-866-979-0447

UNITED KINGDOM AND EUROPE
licensing@concordtheatricals.co.uk
020-7054-7298

No one shall make any changes in this title(s) for the purpose of production. No part of this book may be reproduced, stored in a retrieval system, scanned, uploaded, or transmitted in any form, by any means, now known or yet to be invented, including mechanical, electronic, digital, photocopying, recording, videotaping, or otherwise, without the prior written permission of the publisher. No one shall share this title(s), or any part of this title(s), through any social media or file hosting websites.

For all inquiries regarding motion picture, television, online/digital and other media rights, please contact Concord Theatricals Corp.

MUSIC AND THIRD-PARTY MATERIALS USE NOTE

Licensees are solely responsible for obtaining formal written permission from copyright owners to use copyrighted music and/or other copyrighted third-party materials (e.g. artworks, logos) in the performance of this play and are strongly cautioned to do so. If no such permission is obtained by the licensee, then the licensee must use only original music and materials that the licensee owns and controls. Licensees are solely responsible and liable for clearances of all third-party copyrighted materials, including without limitation music, and shall indemnify the copyright owners of the play(s) and their licensing agent, Concord Theatricals Corp., against any costs, expenses, losses and liabilities arising from the use of such copyrighted third-party materials by licensees. For music, please contact the appropriate music licensing authority in your territory for the rights to any incidental music.

IMPORTANT BILLING AND CREDIT REQUIREMENTS

If you have obtained performance rights to this title, please refer to your licensing agreement for important billing and credit requirements.

the ripple, the wave that carried me home was orignally commissioned and produced by Berkeley Repertory Theatre in association with the Goodman Theatre in Chicago. Developed with support from The Ground Floor at Berkeley Repertory Theatre, Berkeley, California. The co-production opened on September 14, 2022, at Berkeley Rep and ran through October 16, 2022, before transferring to the Goodman Theatre, where it opened on January 23, 2023, and ran through February 12, 2023. It was directed by Jackson Gay, with set design by Todd Rosenthal, costume design by Montana Levi Blanco, hair and wig design by Cookie Jordan, lighting design by Jason Lynch, sound design by Noel Nichols & UptownWorks, movement by Erika Chong Shuch, dramaturgy by Madeleine Oldham. The production stage manager at the Goodman Theatre was Kaitlin Kitzmiller; at Berkeley Rep, Elisa Guthertz. The cast was as follows:

GAYLE/YOUNG CHIPPER AMBITIOUS BLACK WOMAN . . . .
Brianna Buckley

JANICE . . . . Christiana Clark

EDWIN . . . . Ronald L. Conner

HELEN . . . . Aneisa Hicks

CHARACTERS

Although Janice and her family appear at various ages throughout the play, the cast should be around the same age as the person playing Janice. Age range of the company ideally should be 30s–40s.

GAYLE – the aunt, Black American woman

JANICE – the daughter, Black American woman

EDWIN – the father, Black American man

HELEN – the mother, Black American woman

YOUNG CHIPPER AMBITIOUS BLACK WOMAN – late 20s, Black American woman (played by the performer who plays Gayle)

REPORTER, JUROR, CITIZEN – news playing from the television voiced by the actor playing Edwin, understudies, or others

JANICE'S ANSWERING MACHINE – voiced by the performer who plays Edwin or another male voice

HELEN & GAYLE'S ANSWERING MACHINE – voiced by the performer who plays Gayle

SETTING

Beacon, Kansas &
A suburb near a downtown city in Ohio.

TIME

1930s–1992 (the first few days of the LA Riots)

AUTHOR'S NOTES

The pace is swift. Like swimming.
Memory is vigorous; determined. Like swimming.
The storytelling uses every muscle. Like swimming.

Explore Janice's sense of humor. It is present throughout.

The 1992 video footage of the LAPD attacking Rodney King should NOT be shown, projected or played. It is referenced throughout but I do not want the video to be played.

While the play has a fluid relationship with time and age, I've decided to include a timeline on the final page of the script as a reference for the actors. It is my hope the timeline is a thing to consider, not adhere to.

Re: actors playing different ages, it is more important to capture the energy of the age rather than "play" the age. No one should "play" a child in this world. Consider how the eight-year-old version of the adult character exists in the space.

The [=.=] symbol is called "chicken feet." Given the context of the scene, it represents an active moment that transcends words. It can be a gesture, a look, a consideration to say the next line (or the choice to say something different). The duration of the moment should be no longer than a sneeze.

In blackness.

The phone rings.
Rings.

The answering machine steps in:

"You've reached Janice and Winston Clifton.
We're unable to take your call right now.
Leave a message and we'll get back to you as
soon as we can. Blessings."

Beeeeeeep

A **YOUNG CHIPPER AMBITIOUS BLACK WOMAN** *speaks:*

YOUNG CHIPPER AMBITIOUS BLACK WOMAN.   Good morning.

My name is Young Chipper Ambitious Black woman.

And I'm calling on behalf of the African-American Recognition Committee in Beacon, Kansas.

Mrs. Clifton, can you give me a call at your earliest convenience?

I have a thrilling proposition to discuss with you.

I can be reached at 621.655.3323.

Blessings to you both, as well!

(The message ends.
Silence.)

(Time passes.)

The phone rings.
Rings.

The answering machine steps in:

"You've reached Janice and Winston Clifton. We're unable to take your call right now. Leave a message and we'll get back to you as soon as we can. Blessings."

**Beeeeeep*.*

It's **YOUNG CHIPPER AMBITIOUS BLACK WOMAN** *again:*

Hello, Mrs. Clifton.

This is Young Chipper Ambitious Black Woman following up in regards to the message I left you last week.

I have not received a response to my initial reach out, so circling back to you again.

She clears her throat.

My apologies I had a bit of a tickle in my throat.

I am hoping to speak with you soon to discuss a celebration slash event I am organizing here in Beacon.

Once again, my number is 621.655.3323.

Thank you...

The message ends.

Time passes.

The phone rings.
Rings.

The answering machine steps in:

"You've reached Janice and Winston Clifton. We're unable to take your call right now. Leave a message and we'll get back to you as soon as we can. Blessings."

Beeeeeep

GAYLE *speaks:*

GAYLE. Janice.

Will you please return that Young Black Chipper's call?

I have bumped into her several times out in public.

And each time she lets me know you haven't gotten back to her.

Now, you and I are family.

I will not put your business out in the street.

I have no intention of telling her you prefer to keep your time in Beacon to the obligatory minimum, but Young Chipper is a strain of Black etiquette that will pick and pick until her desired outcome is acquired.

And.

I cannot cuss her out because her family owns the complex we now live in.

So.

You see, I fall into an uncomfortable position the longer you fail to return her call and each time I bump into Black Chipper.

=.=

Please relieve all parties of this strain.

=.=

This is Aunt Gayle, by the way. Thank you.

Goodbye.

The message ends.

Lights up on **JANICE**, *mid 30s.*
She holds a glass of water.
She speaks directly to us.

JANICE. In the house I grew up in

I learned to place a glass of water

on my bedside table every night.

In the morning, I'd wake up, sit up in bed,

and down that glass of water as fast as I could.

I hated the taste of water.

I still do.

But we, you and I, each of us are sixty percent water –
give or take a few percentages. You and I need it. In a
way, we are it – water.

"One can say each of us – every man, woman, and small
child – is a small river…"

My family, my ancestry, is a tree of small rivers.

Roots filled with lakes of memory.

So while I grew up in a landlocked environment the
family was an ocean.

=.=

I sit on that lone branch that yearns for the sturdiness
of land.

I don't like water.

I hate the way it feels against my skin.

The way it soaks my hair, splashes against my scalp.

I am sixty percent water.

=.=

=.=

It is morning.

She drinks the glass of water.

A workday, a school day in the middle of March.

1992.

Winston is downstairs making breakfast for the boys.

I am upstairs in the shower worrying about what needs to be tackled at the office. I run all administrative responsibilities for alumni relations at a small college in Ohio. The institution has a reputation of a decent science school. Many of the students go on to be dentists, podiatrists, and optometrists. I facilitate reunion committees, ask campaigns, and help design "enthusiasm packages."

My job is basically, reminding people to come back and give back.

This year, we have yet to hit our target number of donations. And it doesn't look like we will.

There's a knock at the bathroom door.

It's my youngest: Nate.

He cracks open the door to tell me Young Black Chipper has left another message.

Why does this heifer keep calling me?

And that means another call from Aunt Gayle isn't far behind.

There's an unspoken, longstanding agreement that phone calls with my people in Beacon occur on the following occasions:

– the first and third Sundays of each month
– seven of the ten government holidays

– immediate family birthdays
– minor surgeries and subsequent periods of healing.

All of Winston's family is based here in Ohio, so I've tucked the boys neatly into that circle.

When the oldest was a baby, we drove to Kansas for a visit.

The youngest has never been.

We rarely spend time in Beacon.

I've always made arrangements for my parents to visit us in Ohio.

When my daddy died a few years ago, I chose to go alone to the funeral. Winston didn't agree with that choice, but he respected it.

I married him for several reasons: love, his beauty, strength, tenderness, and the fact that he trusted I knew what was best when it came to my side of the family.

=.=

Water is a complicated element.

It heals, destroys, rescues, erases.

It drowns. It saves.

It holds memory. It washes away pain.

Vacations at the beach now, I sit on the shore. Watch like a tourist as my husband plays with the boys in the ocean. I see their joy but cannot hear it. The wind and rolling waves silence their laughter and squeals.

I look at them, never knowing that joy. I inherited the weight of water. The heaviness, the consequence of it – not the joy.

=.=

March 1956.

There are three public pools in Beacon, Kansas.

Brookside is for the Negroes.

The Gregory Lane and SunRay are <u>not</u>.

The Gregory Lane is <u>the</u> finest swimming experience the city offered white folks.

A tank the length of six Cadillacs, concrete decks, and plush grassy lawns.

SunRay wasn't as nice, but was far from pathetic.

Brookside was located in a Black neighborhood occupied by folks who were referred to as the "Thinking Class."

Thinking Class Blacks meaning middle-class families.

My mama's side of the family lived in this neighborhood.

Years prior the family petitioned the city to build a pool demanding Negroes had just as much right as the white folks to recreate.

To subdue the "evil consequences of integration," the city built Brookside.

It wasn't as nice as SunRay, but it was clean and respectable. A symbol of achievement. My grandfather gave Black children free swim lessons every summer.

It was a time when every young person in Beacon could learn how to swim.

Enter my daddy, Edwin Collen.

Faint light on **EDWIN** *in his mid-30s.*

...whose family was <u>not</u> a part of the Thinking Class.

Daddy lived with the Black folks who didn't have the clout to get anything built, maintained, or even considered.

In his part of Beacon, people could only afford necessities.

No one went to bed hungry, but their circumstance defined their neighborhood –

The Necessity Class.

My grandfather taught all the children in Thinking Class how to swim. And as a gesture of goodwill, he wanted to offer lessons to The Necessities. He got his church, the largest Black church in Beacon, to use its van to transport young Necessity people to Brookside. My grandfather, being a descendant of the church founder, made this possible even when many in the congregation were against it.

This was an example of the clout Mama's family had and how they used it.

Daddy, eight years old, took the van from his neighborhood, rode past The Gregory Lane and SunRay, to learn how to float in Brookside. Unbeknownst to anyone at the time, his future father-in-law (my grandfather) taught him how.

My mama Helen at fourteen.

Faint light on **HELEN** *in her mid-30s.*

Throughout her teens she studied Latin, ballet, and piano. During swim season, she gave lessons to little kids whose parents didn't know how to swim, or were too afraid of the water.

Light rises fully on **HELEN**, *as she shifts into a teen. She pantomimes a typical lesson.*

HELEN. That's it. You're doing fine...

JANICE. Edwin, in his teens, tested the boundaries of authority. He spent most summers daydreaming of takeovers at The Gregory Lane pool. It was closer to his neighborhood than Brookside.

So close he could hear the water splash and melodies of delight from those who were allowed to enter.

A few times, he rallied friends and walked to the entrance.

> *Light rises fully on* **EDWIN**, *standing at the entrance as a teen. He holds out coins.*

EDWIN. There were often five of us. Sometimes only two.

We stood there in our trunks and tees. Polite. Patient.

JANICE. *(Quotes the gatekeeper.)* "No Negroes here. Brookside only."

HELEN. That's a good job!

See? I told you: the water is your friend.

Your kicks are so good!

> *Lights out on* **HELEN**.

JANICE. The Gregory Lane was impenetrable. Fencing around the perimeter and lifeguards who did the double duty of pool security.

With so much effort put into protecting Gregory Lane, it left the SunRay pool vulnerable.

> **EDWIN**, *in his 30s, tells a young* **JANICE**
> *the story.*
> *He* <u>*loves*</u> *telling this story.*

EDWIN. SunRay wouldn't let us in either.

But it didn't have as many ways to keep us out.

JANICE. *(To us.)* Just shy of his eighteenth birthday...

EDWIN. *(To* **JANICE**.*)* I had memorized the best ways onto the grounds and the fastest way out.

All without being detected.

Even now, you could blindfold me, drop me there in the dead of night, and I could find my way out in record time – no trouble at all.

JANICE. *(To us.)*   **EDWIN**. *(To **JANICE**.)*
There were four of 'em...   There were four of us...

EDWIN. *(To **JANICE**.)* My best friend Franklin.

Your uncle Dougie.

And our cousin Reggie: who was the Sugar Chile *(Rhymes with "smile".)* Robinson of swimming.

JANICE. ...I don't know who Sugar Chile is, daddy...

EDWIN. You don't? (**JANICE** *shakes her head.*)

I never played you his music?

> *Another head shake from* **JANICE**.

I'll have to change that...

The point is Reggie was a water prodigy.

He was born by a river –

JANICE. Just like Sam Cooke!

EDWIN. *(Can't help but chuckle.)* Well...yea...sorta like Sam Cooke.

But Reggie could swim any current, any temperature, for any distance.

He breathed two elements: air and water.

If Black folks could compete in that part of the Olympics, he'd have a whole house filled with medals and trophies. Stadiums would be named in his honor.

He was super bad. And a solid cat, too.

Back then he was slim and strong and quick. A few years younger than me.

I told him what I wanted to do at SunRay, he was on board just like that.

It was going down.

The four of us snuck in on a hot summer day.

I stood by the way out.

Franklin was by the way in.

And Dougie was at the meeting spot with a dry set of clothes.

Stationed at our marks, Reggie stripped down to his trunks.

Franklin, on the lookout, counted off:

One

Two

Three!

!!!POW!!!

Reggie zoomed straight for that tank of water!

All muscle, power, and revolution!

He stuck to the route I mapped out, so he had a clear shot.

Then: SPLASH!!!

He's in the water!!!

White folks scream and holler.

Women scramble to get out while fellas jump in and try to get a hold of that beautiful, Black Aquaman!

Towels flail. Pool toys tossed in the air.

In the chaos, Reggie stayed on task:

Moves his arms in freestyle swim stroke.

He makes it to the other end of the pool.

He jumps out and jets towards me.

My heart matches his pace.

Angry red faces not far behind, but Poseidon was on our side that day.

He and I jet down a zigzag, juke-style path.

And we got away. They couldn't catch us.

We got away.

> **EDWIN** *is slightly winded.*
> *The joy of the memory, mixed with pride,*
> *mixed with adrenaline.*

JANICE. Did you ever get in trouble?

EDWIN. They never found out it was us.

The story made the paper and everything.

But no one snitched.

SunRay got shut down for three whole days.

JANICE. Why?

EDWIN. Sanitization.

A Negro "infected" the water they said.

So the city drained the tank, steam cleaned it, then filled it back up –

> *The phone in 1992 rings.*

> *Shift.* **JANICE** *returns to the present of 1992.*

> *The answering machine steps in:*

> *"You've reached Janice and Winston Clifton.*
> *We're unable to take your call right now.*

Leave a message and we'll get back to you as soon as we can. Blessings."

**Beeeeeep*.*

It's **YOUNG CHIPPER AMBITIOUS BLACK WOMAN**, *a bit less courteous:*

YOUNG CHIPPER AMBITIOUS BLACK WOMAN. Hello, Mrs. Clifton.

This is Young Chipper Ambitious Black Woman following up…again.

Your Aunt Gayle mentioned how busy you are up there in…Ohio,

but I implore: please find a moment to reach me…

JANICE. Winston is afraid Young Chipper will appear at the front door if I don't return her call.

I plan to contact her from the office – to provide myself an easy out if necessary.

But the days are busy and the evenings are spent helping the boys with homework.

By the time night rolls around –

> *Mid 1960s,* **HELEN** *and* **EDWIN** *at home after a long day.*
> *Husband and wife, both in their 30s.* **EDWIN** *collapses next to* **HELEN**, *exhausted.*

EDWIN. I am exhausted.

HELEN. She's asleep?

EDWIN. She's asleep.

Finally.

Took longer than usual.

And that tantrum at dinner…

HELEN. She had a tough day.

EDWIN. It's third grade.

What's tough?

HELEN. She got into a fight.

EDWIN. A fight?

HELEN. It wasn't a big deal.

EDWIN. With who?

HELEN. A boy –

EDWIN. A boy?!

HELEN. They're eight, baby.

It's not like Janice was fighting Ali.

EDWIN. Why didn't you tell me?

HELEN. I'm telling you now.

EDWIN. Helen...

HELEN. I went up to the school. Talked to the principal.

Brought her home. She's frightened more than anything.

She didn't want to disappoint you.

EDWIN. That explains dinner.

And bedtime.

It's been a year since she asked me to read her a story.

Tonight, it was like she didn't want me to leave her side.

What was the fight about?

HELEN. The boy splashed water at Janice's best friend.

The friend cried. Janice told him to apologize.

He wouldn't. They argued. Wrestled.

EDWIN. Wow…

HELEN. Yea…

Our baby's executing

some of that street justice.

EDWIN. I know, right?

She can put that energy into the BT this year.

HELEN. Why would Janice need energy for the BT Remembrance?

EDWIN. Well… I was thinking…this might be a good year for her to get more…involved in the events.

Maybe…say a few words at the opening ceremony.

She could read a poem, or you could write a little speech for her.

HELEN. Baby, I… I don't think that's a good idea.

EDWIN. Why not?

HELEN. She's eight years old.

EDWIN. Old enough to be a vigilante…

HELEN. It's not a joke, Edwin. The first year you want her to speak, she's eight years old.

Janice is the same age as those boys who drowned.

EDWIN. =.=

HELEN. Don't tell me you didn't know that.

EDWIN. I'm not gonna lie. I did.

But that's what makes it so powerful, baby.

We've been hosting this event before Janice was even born.

And we do it to honor the Beacon Three and protest the public pool closures.

This year, our daughter can stand at that microphone to symbolize what our community has lost and remind us what we're fighting for.

=.=

=.=

I'll ask her if she wants to do it.

HELEN. If <u>you</u> ask, she'll do it. For you.

You know that.

EDWIN. I'll be as neutral as possible.

> *Shift.*
> **JANICE** *in the present of 1992.*
> *To us:*

JANICE. Those three boys that drowned? It happened March 1956.

March third to be exact.

There were four of 'em: Two white boys. Two Black.

They were friends and wanted to swim together.

Could they go to Gregory Lane? SunRay? No.

And while Brookside never explicitly said "no whites."

Neither Black boy could recall seeing one there.

One of them remembered a lake on the edge of Beacon.

They set out on foot, à la "Stand by Me."

Eight years old.

But only one came back.

=.=

The others became known as the Beacon Three...

=.=

The tragedy was significant on its own, but it charged the fight to end segregated city pools in Beacon.

My parents played a role in persuading Necessity Blacks to unite with Thinking Blacks for the first time in the city's history.

And they got several well-meaning Gregory Lane patrons to join the cause as well.

A year later, 1957, a judge ruled all tanks open to anyone who had money to pay.

As soon as his gavel smacked against the bench confirming his decision, mobs gathered to guard Gregory and SunRay – determined to keep swimming "pure."

Black children who approached with legal tender in hand were chased away with rocks and sticks.

Teenagers punched.

Men beaten, stabbed.

Even Black folks who walked <u>near</u> the neighborhoods were harassed.

Attacks became common at all three locations.

Attendance dropped.

And in 1958, just as I entered the world, the city shut down all pools.

Swimming became a social and political symbol.

Water turned into denial, rejection.

=.=

Brookside was no more.

The swim program my granddaddy operated for almost fifteen years ended.

With no access many children never learned to swim.

Mama was determined I learn, so when I was a toddler, we began the forty-five-minute weekly drives to the neighboring city that would grant us access to an indoor facility.

> **HELEN** *pantomimes giving young* **JANICE** *swim lessons.*

HELEN. That's it, my love. You're doing fine...

See? I told you: the water is your friend...

> *Return to* **JANICE** *in the present 1992.*

JANICE. Water was my friend...

=.=

I started speaking at the BT event when I was eight.

My father asked me. I couldn't say no...

> **EDWIN** *appears.*

EDWIN. Baby girl, isn't it sad what happened to those boys?

JANICE. Yes.

EDWIN. Do you think it's important for the community to honor those boys?

JANICE. Yes.

EDWIN. And who's a part of the community?

JANICE. =.=

EDWIN. Me, Mama, Uncle Dougie...who else?

JANICE. People at church.

EDWIN. That's right. Who else...?

JANICE. The Youngs next door.

The Washingtons down the street. Everybody in our neighborhood.

EDWIN. Yes! And...

JANICE. =.=

EDWIN. =.=

JANICE. =.=

EDWIN. You.

JANICE. =.=

EDWIN. You're a part of this community.

JANICE. =.=

Okay...

EDWIN. And as a part of this community that honors its people, you can choose how you want to show your support.

JANICE. =.=

EDWIN. How do you show your support to someone you know?

JANICE. But I don't know those boys, daddy.

They died before I was even born.

EDWIN. Well, someone you care about.

How do you show your support even if you don't know them?

JANICE. *(To us.)* Even now, as a grown woman, I can't answer this question in a way that feels authentic to me.

EDWIN. *(Speaking to the young* **JANICE.***)* You can use your voice, baby girl.

Your voice is such a powerful tool.

To speak up for those who cannot speak.

> *Shift.*
> *In 1992,* **JANICE** *speaks to us.*

JANICE. I ended up speaking every year until I was fifteen.

I can't remember any of the speeches I gave at those events.

I can't remember all the rallies, the marches from my childhood…

But I do remember those moments of unity I felt with my parents.

> **JANICE**, *a pre-teen, at home with* **EDWIN** *and* **HELEN** *in the late 1960s.*
> *This familiar protest chant quickly morphs into a freestyle word game that always manages to make them laugh…*

(Chant.) Our people

united

will never be defeated…

JANICE, HELEN & EDWIN. *(Chant.)* Our people

united

will never be defeated…

JANICE. Our people

like-minded

would never be

elitist.

EDWIN. The beagle

near-sighted

could never be conceited.

HELEN. The seagulls

excited

could get

overheated.

JANICE. Dung beetles

bronchitis

they need proper treatment...

A shared laugh among the three shifts into 1992. **JANICE** *at work on the phone with:*

Note: although their exchange is a phone call, **YOUNG CHIPPER AMBITIOUS BLACK WOMAN** *should be present onstage during this scene.*

YOUNG CHIPPER AMBITIOUS BLACK WOMAN. Mrs. Clifton, I can't tell you how wonderful it is to hear your voice.

JANICE. I'm so sorry it's taken me some time to return your call, Young Chipper...

YOUNG CHIPPER AMBITIOUS BLACK WOMAN. That is quite alright.

You have a very full plate.

You know, my second cousin got his dentistry degree from your school.

JANICE. Did he?

YOUNG CHIPPER AMBITIOUS BLACK WOMAN. Yes, he's doing very well for himself.

He opened a practice here in Beacon.

And I get my cleanings at a discount, hallelujah.

(Polite laughter.)

JANICE. It helps to have family in high places.

YOUNG CHIPPER AMBITIOUS BLACK WOMAN. With the cost of dental insurance? Indeed.

You know, Mrs. Clifton, I promised once I got you on the phone, I wouldn't take up too much time, so let me get right to it.

JANICE. Alright...

YOUNG CHIPPER AMBITIOUS BLACK WOMAN. As you well know, Beacon has a very complicated history around segregation and racial politics.

JANICE. "Complicated"...?

YOUNG CHIPPER AMBITIOUS BLACK WOMAN. Yes, but we also have such a rich history of trailblazers who helped steer us Beconians to the right side of justice and equality.

As you may also know, I am chairing the African-American Recognition Committee. And since accepting this position, I've really tried to guide us into a more dynamic and robust showing of support and honoring our community members.

With that said, your father Edwin Collen, Jr. was <u>such</u> an active and vital part of Beacon's history.

Particularly around advocacy and public space.

And he really galvanized Black people's pride and excellence in aquatic pursuits.

JANICE. *(...But.)* My mother as well.

YOUNG CHIPPER AMBITIOUS BLACK WOMAN. Excuse me?

JANICE. My mother was just as active as my dad.

YOUNG CHIPPER AMBITIOUS BLACK WOMAN. Of course... but Mr. Collen played such a role in becoming the <u>face</u> of the movement.

JANICE. =.=

Is this getting uncomfortable?
YOUNG CHIPPER AMBITIOUS BLACK WOMAN *isn't sure, so she decides to press on.*

YOUNG CHIPPER AMBITIOUS BLACK WOMAN. With that knowledge of history, I am thrilled to report the board has agreed to rename the indoor swimming facility in the Thinking area of Beacon.

It will now be known as The Edwin P. Collen, Jr. Pool.

JANICE. =.=

YOUNG CHIPPER AMBITIOUS BLACK WOMAN. =.=

JANICE. =.=

YOUNG CHIPPER AMBITIOUS BLACK WOMAN. Mrs. Clifton?

JANICE. Yes. I'm here.

YOUNG CHIPPER AMBITIOUS BLACK WOMAN. =.=

=.=

And. Well. We planned a really lovely naming ceremony.

And, we wondered if you might want to attend

and say a few words?

To honor your father?

JANICE. =.=

YOUNG CHIPPER AMBITIOUS BLACK WOMAN. Mrs. Clifton?

JANICE. When is the ceremony?

YOUNG CHIPPER AMBITIOUS BLACK WOMAN. Well, we'd like for it to happen on the same date your father reopened the Brookside pool in 1979.

JANICE. April 30th.

YOUNG CHIPPER AMBITIOUS BLACK WOMAN. Yes!

=.=

Could you attend?

JANICE. =.=

YOUNG CHIPPER AMBITIOUS BLACK WOMAN. It will be a really wonderful day.

You can bring your family –

JANICE. I wouldn't.

YOUNG CHIPPER AMBITIOUS BLACK WOMAN. ???

JANICE. It's my mother-in-law's birthday.

There's a big party every year.

YOUNG CHIPPER AMBITIOUS BLACK WOMAN. Oooo, that does sound like fun.

Does this mean <u>you</u> won't be able to attend?

JANICE. =.=

Can I think about it?

YOUNG CHIPPER AMBITIOUS BLACK WOMAN. Of course.

Yes.

Can you give me your answer by next week?

JANICE. Yes.

YOUNG CHIPPER AMBITIOUS BLACK WOMAN. Great!

Mrs. Clifton, thank you so much for your time.

I hope I wasn't too greedy.

JANICE. Not at all...

YOUNG CHIPPER AMBITIOUS BLACK WOMAN. I'll be in touch soon.

Blessings...

> *March 1956.*
> **EDWIN** *and* **HELEN** *in their early 20s.*
> *Outdoors in the Thinking area of Beacon.*
> *Both are dressed in funeral clothes.*

HELEN. Those caskets were so small.

And to watch them lowered into the ground...

EDWIN. Heartbreaking.

HELEN. It was nice they were able to bury the two of them next to each other.

EDWIN. Yes.

HELEN. Have you heard anything else about the third funeral?

EDWIN. The pastor said it'll be tomorrow.

At Mt. Calvary.

The boy's mother extended an invitation...

HELEN. But the father retracted it.

I heard.

Why can't we mourn together?

How can we be separate in the face of this tragedy?

All three of those boys should've been buried together.

EDWIN. We don't have a cemetery that allows that...

HELEN. And no one asks why?

EDWIN. =.=

=.=

We should get back for the repass.

The one we <u>can</u> attend.

HELEN. =.=

=.=

I need a few more moments.

> **EDWIN** *sits with* **HELEN**.
> *Holds her. They comfort each other.*

I'm such a coward...

EDWIN. Why?

HELEN. I'm afraid to go to the repass.

EDWIN. I'll be with you.

Hold your hand.

HELEN. I can't even look them in the eye.

EDWIN. Who?

HELEN. The mothers.

I... I managed brief hugs, but I can't find any words.

EDWIN. Every moment doesn't call for words, love.

Sometimes a hug and a kind hand is all that's needed.

HELEN. =.=

EDWIN. =.=

HELEN. I keep thinking about those boys...drowning.

To be that young and have to fight...

To be that small...the possibility of survival is...

EDWIN. I think about them, too.

HELEN. You do?

EDWIN. Yes. How couldn't I?

Anyone with a heart, a soul has to.

HELEN. The parents can't swim.

EDWIN. No?

HELEN. And to lose a child by drowning...

=.=

I taught both of those boys.

They took lessons with me three summers ago...

EDWIN. =.=

HELEN. Right at Brookside pool.

My hands held just beneath them as they floated...

=.=

And now I can't look their mothers in the eye.

EDWIN. Helen, what happened to them wasn't your fault.

That lake is dangerous even for the fish, let alone kids.

All that trash that gets tossed in it – no wonder one of them got tangled up. Those three boys tried to save each other, I'm sure of it.

HELEN. Why is that lake so accessible anyway?

The city spends hundreds to put up fences and guards at Gregory Lane, but at that lake there's just a rusted, faded metal sign dangling from a broken chain.

=.=

This one time I went,

there was a car in it.

Somebody pushed a whole car.

You could see the rusted roof poking up from the surface.

Like a crocodile –

EDWIN. Who were you there with?

HELEN. What?

EDWIN. That one time you went to the lake.

Who all was there?

HELEN. Why?

EDWIN. I think that's a valid question

for a fiancé to ask his girl.

HELEN. Eddie, I was a teenager.

EDWIN. Even so...

HELEN. Have <u>you</u> been to that lake?

EDWIN. Sure.

HELEN. Well, who'd you go with?

EDWIN.	**HELEN.**
That's different!	And don't you dare say it's different!

HELEN. You took girls there, didn't you?

EDWIN. *(Coy?)* Maybe one or two.

HELEN. Well I went with one or two fellas.

And that's my right, my duty.

EDWIN. Is it?

HELEN. As an experienced swimmer and lifeguard, yes.

EDWIN. It was that goofy looking guy who plays drums at the church, wasn't it?

HELEN. Eddie, this isn't the time

to quibble over past endeavors.

=.=

I want to do something about that lake.

EDWIN. Like what?

HELEN. Make it so people can't be in it.

Or clean it so that it's safe.

We have to honor those boys.

The tragedy of the loss.

If we continue on as usual, what have we learned?

EDWIN. Is this your first time in America?

Let me show you around...

HELEN. Eddie...

EDWIN. Darling, this country <u>is built</u> on selective memory.

We spend most of our time reminding people we're human.

One of the victims was that white boy,

that's the only reason the story was even in the paper.

HELEN. Why not take advantage of that?

EDWIN. Of what?

HELEN. If his race gets the attention, we should use it to make real change.

His mother invited the other two mothers to the funeral, right?

EDWIN. Right.

HELEN. Which means she has a fair amount of compassion, reason –

EDWIN. That's a lot of conclusion you're digging up...

HELEN. Can you not be a pill for one moment?

If you don't believe in this city, this country,

can you believe in me?

EDWIN. =.=

HELEN. I want to change how a tiny part of the system works, Eddie.

What's wrong with wanting that?

EDWIN. Nothing's wrong with that, darling.

> **HELEN** *exits in annoyance.* **EDWIN** *goes after her. Calls out:*

Helen...aww, come on. You know I believe in you...

> **JANICE** *in the present of 1992.*

JANICE. I tell Winston about the ceremony,

about renaming the facility in my father's name.

I ask him what he thinks.

I love and respect the way my husband's mind connects with his emotions.

He often has a much more balanced view.

In so many ways he reminds me of the successfulness of my parents as a unit.

As an adult, I admire the unit Edwin and Helen cultivated.

But growing up, I often felt left out of their pairing.

=.=

I knew I wanted to marry Winston the first time he and I went on a camping trip.

He's the only Black Eagle Scout I've ever met.

And I loved watching him navigate and negotiate with the land.

And I loved how we worked together with the land.

I was not a girl scout. Everything I learned was from Aunt Gayle and Uncle Bobby –

they had a farm back in the day. I spent a summer there when I was seventeen.

I found peace that summer.

And Winston rekindled that peace when we were sophomores in college.

=.=

The fact that Winston and I are a team...that's important to me.

=.=

He thinks I should attend the ceremony.

Say a few words.

He thinks it's an incredible honor.

=.=

I can't help but feel like that eight-year-old, sitting with my daddy when he asks me to speak at the BT Remembrance.

I did it for him. I do it for him. Even though I'm unsure if it's something I want.

=.=

But sometimes doing the right thing calls for –

(**EDWIN** *rushes on...*)

EDWIN. *(Calls out.)* Baby girl!!

> *(He crosses to the record player, excited. Places the needle on the record. A song in the style of "Go Boy Go" by Sugar Chile Robinson begins.*)*

---

*A license to produce THE RIPPLE, THE WAVE THAT CARRIED ME HOME does not include a performance license for "Go Boy Go." The publisher and author suggest that the licensee contact ASCAP or BMI to ascertain the music publisher and contact such music publisher to license or acquire permission for performance of the song. If a license or permission is unattainable for "Go Boy Go," the licensee may not use the song in THE RIPPLE, THE WAVE THAT CARRIED ME HOME but should create an original composition in a similar style or use a similar song in the public domain. For further information, please see the Music and Third-Party Materials Use Note on page iii.

(Calls out.) Baby girl, come here!

> JANICE, *a pre-teen, appears.* EDWIN, *giddy, dances to the music.*

JANICE. Daddy, what are you doing?

EDWIN. **This is Sugar Chile Robinson!**

> EDWIN, *dancing, reaches for* JANICE*'s hand. She is shy in a typical pre-teen way, but her father coaxes joy from her.*
>
> *Soon, they're both playfully dancing to the music.*
>
> HELEN *appears,* EDWIN *tries to bring her in, but she shoos him away. Wants to watch her daughter and husband dance.*
>
> *The song slows, taking on a dreamy quality.*
>
> JANICE *continues to dance, oblivious to the change in the music.*
>
> EDWIN *stops dancing.* HELEN *stops dancing. Both exit.*
>
> JANICE *suddenly realizes she's alone. She stops dancing.*
>
> *In the present moment of 1992.*
>
> JANICE *gets on the phone. She dials a number. The phone rings.*
>
> *Finally, the answering machine kicks in:*
>
> *"You reached 621.878.7839. Please leave a message."*

Beeeeeep

JANICE. Hello…

Aunt Gayle…

I know somebody's there.

Pick up, pick up, pick up. It's Janice.

> *(A moment passes.*
> *Then a rustling of the receiver.)*

GAYLE. Hello?

Feedback.

Let me…

Feedback.

Hold on.

> **GAYLE** *stops the answering machine from*
> *amplifying their voices.*

Hello?

JANICE. Hi.

GAYLE. Are you watching this trial?

JANICE. What trial?

GAYLE. What trial?!

The Rodney King trial.

Court TV is covering it.

This cable bill cuts into my wine budget,

but it's worth it.

JANICE. Do you need money?

I can cover the cable bill.

GAYLE. No, no, your mother would

never let that happen.

She'd talk so bad about me:

watching this trial _and_ being able

to enjoy my Merlot.

JANICE. You want me to call you back?

GAYLE. No, no. I tape it for your mother.

I can watch it tonight with her.

Why are you calling?

Did something happen?

JANICE. Where's Mama?

GAYLE. Volunteering at the elementary cafeteria.

That's something she does now.

JANICE. Why aren't you down there with her?

GAYLE. Me witnessing this trial is my contribution

to the community.

I hope those cops get what they deserve.

Don't make no sense.

Did you see that video?

JANICE. I saw the video…

GAYLE. They look so smug, too. Those cops.

Like they know they'll be acquitted.

I swear, putting my hope in the justice system is like
paying church tithes.

It gets the pastor a new suit, but doesn't do a thing

to ease my suffering.

JANICE. Are you usually this cheerful in the day?

GAYLE. I put on my happy face every morning.

You calling from work?

JANICE. Yes.

GAYLE. Who's sick?

JANICE. Nobody's sick.

GAYLE. So why the phone call?

JANICE. I finally spoke to Young Chipper.

GAYLE. She told you about the naming ceremony.

JANICE. Yes.

GAYLE. And.

JANICE. And?

GAYLE. Are you coming?

JANICE. Maybe.

I think so. Yea.

GAYLE. So much enthusiasm…

JANICE. Are you gonna be there?

Will Mama be there?

GAYLE. Of course.

Where else would we be?

We're both retired widows. We have no excuse to be anywhere else when someone invites us to anything.

JANICE. I have a serious question.

GAYLE. What's that?

JANICE. Shouldn't they name that facility after Mama <u>and</u> Daddy?

GAYLE. =.=

JANICE. Or your side of the family?

Or...maybe name it after Mama?

GAYLE. Why would they do that?

JANICE. You know the history just as well as I do.

Even better. You were around for most of it.

GAYLE. Your daddy was more of the face of things.

JANICE. That's what Young Chipper said.

GAYLE. The Kings have clout. Your mama could

get the meetings and the financing.

But your father –

JANICE. Isn't that the most important part?

The connections? The money?

GAYLE. Is this your first time in America?

Let me show you around...

JANICE. Aunt Gayle...

GAYLE. Janice, no one is interested in who <u>funds</u> change;

who pulled strings.

People remember the faces on the front line;

the man who stood on the soapbox.

JANICE. What does Mama think about it?

GAYLE. Ask her.

JANICE. =.=

GAYLE. You should talk to her.

JANICE. =.=

GAYLE. And not the usual Sunday polites.

=.=

You left your daddy's funeral with barely a word of substance –

JANICE. Aunt Gayle...

GAYLE. I'm just saying...

JANICE. I understand...

GAYLE. Do you?

JANICE. =.=

GAYLE. It's the right thing to do.

JANICE. =.=

GAYLE. That's what your mama thinks.

Going to the ceremony is the right thing to do.

=.=

We all know your parents were a team.

We all know how they worked together to get things done in Beacon.

JANICE. But what about when we're all gone?

That building will hold Daddy's name.

History will hold only his name.

Who will be around to remind folks of Mama?

GAYLE. Don't forget our name still stands strong around here.

The King family name is on the "founding members" plaque at the church.

Your granddaddy's picture still hangs in city hall.

Our side of the family has resonance in memory and stone.

JANICE. =.=

GAYLE. =.=

How are the boys?

JANICE. They're good.

Winston is good. He just got a promotion.

GAYLE. Good... I'm glad.

Still in the same department?

JANICE. A different department,

but the same insurance company.

GAYLE. Okay, good...

Send them kisses.

JANICE. I will.

GAYLE. And how are you?

JANICE. This ceremony is pulling up a lot of memories.

=.=

How are you?

GAYLE. Face them.

The memories.

Don't run from them.

JANICE. That's always your advice: face it.

GAYLE. And when have I been wrong?

JANICE. =.=

GAYLE. That's right...

=.=

Everything's fine here.

I'm fine.

Should I tell your mama you called?

JANICE. =.=

Yes.

GAYLE. Will do.

> *Shift.*
> **JANICE** *speaks to us.*

JANICE. I am fifteen years old.

Seated in the passenger seat – <u>early</u> on a Saturday morning.

I am used to these weekly trips.

They happen from the time I'm a toddler.

Mama wakes me up at dawn to make the forty-five-minute drive to that Olympic-size pool.

As my swimming improves there are fewer instructions from her.

When I am fifteen, we spend an hour doing laps. Perfecting strokes.

It isn't long before I feel stronger than her.

My lungs feel deeper.

My limbs longer.

I keep this feeling to myself.

And then...then we are turned away. No laps that Saturday.

It is on this day, I find out, Mama is friends with the facilities manager.

He lets us swim in the pool before it opens for the white patrons.

We are not allowed inside during formal hours.

I am embarrassed. For myself? Mama? Our Blackness? The ignorance of folks who won't let us swim freely?

We are just as strong and swift and skilled as any other who glides into the pool during formal hours.

> *In 1973* **HELEN** *drives in silence. Angry.* **JANICE** *sits next to her, continues to speak to us.*

I think of Daddy's cousin...

> **EDWIN** *appears in the throes of telling the story about his cousin.*

EDWIN. Reggie zoomed straight for that tank of water!

All muscle, power, and revolution!

JANICE. Mister Facilities Manager greeted us quietly every Saturday.

Red hair cut close – an army buzz cut. A veteran.

He exchanges hushed good mornings.

He asks me about school.

I respond politely every time.

> **HELEN**, *driving, glances in the rearview mirror.*

EDWIN. White folks scream and holler.

SPLASH!!!

He's in the water!!!

JANICE. The silence echoes as Mama and I approach the large tank.

As we walk, the squeaks of our bare feet along the deck mimic bird chirps.

Helen and I slip into the water.

It is warm. Peaceful. Familiar.

> **HELEN**, *driving, sees in the rearview mirror the patrol car following her car.*

EDWIN. Towels flail. Pool toys tossed in the air.

In the chaos, Reggie stayed on task:

Moves his arms in freestyle swim stroke.

JANICE. We reach the hour.

We climb up and out. Only our breath betrays exertion.

Still no words. Only breath and bodies toweling off.

A mother and daughter privileged(?) / lucky(?) enough to have access to this pastime.

> **EDWIN** *shifts away.*
>
> *We're with* **JANICE** *and* **HELEN** *in the car.* **HELEN** *is taut.*
>
> **JANICE** *takes little notice of her mother's energy.*

Did you know cousin Reggie?

HELEN. *(Distracted.)* Hmm?

JANICE. Daddy's cousin Reggie.

The really good swimmer.

Do you know where he is now?

HELEN. I don't, darling.

You can ask your daddy when we get home.

JANICE. =.=

=.=

Are we coming back next week?

HELEN. I don't know.

JANICE. =.=

HELEN. He'll call us. Let us know either way.

=.=

He's a nice man. Mr. Facilities.

=.=

It's been a good place for you and I to go. But that may change.

He's considerate of our safety.

=.=

He'll call us.

JANICE. Is he in trouble?

HELEN. No. He's just being considerate.

> **HELEN** *checks the speedometer.*
> *She then looks into the rearview mirror. The patrol car still follows.*

(*Mutters to herself.*) What is it you want, you cracker bastard?

JANICE. Mama...?

> **JANICE** *looks to her mother. Finally notices the stiffness, the gaze.*
> **JANICE** *sits up to look out the back window.*

HELEN. Janice, no.

There's nothing to see.

Sit back.

JANICE. What is it?

HELEN. A patrol car.

But it's alright, Janice.

Just sit back.

> **JANICE** *sits back.*
> *She looks at the side view mirror.*

> **JANICE** *seated in the car 1973 but speaks to us as herself in the present of 1992.*

JANICE. *(To us.)* I remember this moment in 1973.

Early Saturday morning.

Even as a grown woman in 1992.

After my conversation with Aunt Gayle, I buy a newspaper and read the latest

about The Rodney King trial.

I remember this moment in 1973.

> *Patrol car lights flash.*

HELEN. *(Mutters.)* Shit…

> **HELEN** *slows then stops the car.*

(To **JANICE.***)* We'll be alright.

JANICE. *(To us.)* This feels more like a plea,

a prayer, a call to manifest.

Will it change now? In 1992?

There is evidence, proof, documentation of assault.

King struck and kicked.

Hands and knees against the cold, concrete.

Under bright lights.

King is struck. There is footage.

There is proof. His hand reaches out.

The anchorman on the TV warns us:

"Graphic footage. Viewer discretion advised."

But it is <u>truth</u>, <u>evidence</u>, Mr. Brokaw – the proof <u>will</u> be, <u>must be</u> televised.

In 1973, we are two – a mother and daughter seated in our family car.

Silent, just like past Saturdays.

My mother's calm breath is out of step with my shallow pace.

We will never talk about what happened after that officer asked my mother to step out of the car. She will never know what I saw.

A mother, a daughter will never share the anger, shame, the fear, the worry.

I sweat now in the moment and the <u>memory</u> of the moment.

Driving us home afterwards, my mother looks so calm.

> *Suddenly at home, in 1973.*
> **JANICE** *and* **HELEN** *returned and have just*
> *told* **EDWIN** *about the pullover.*

EDWIN. Did they make you get out of the car?

HELEN. Yes.

EDWIN. Did they give a reason?

HELEN. Do they need a reason?

EDWIN. Helen…

HELEN. They said they've had robberies.

The shops in the area have been vandalized.

EDWIN. Morning robberies?

Who loots at six in the morning?

HELEN. They checked the car.

EDWIN. Two Black women are robbing their stores? What were their names?

(*To* **JANICE.**) Did you see their badges?

HELEN. Go upstairs, Janice.

> **JANICE** *doesn't even protest, she gets up and*
> *exits the scene.*
> *She stands at the edge and watches her*
> *parents.*

(Tempered.) Baby, I need you to calm down.

Okay?

I don't need my husband walking into a precinct to yell
at a bunch of white men with guns.

> **EDWIN** *meets his wife's gaze.*
> *silently, knowingly, she gets him to calm*
> *down. His breath eventually matches her*
> *pace.*

Janice is fine. I'll be...fine.

They just tried to scare us. That's all.

EDWIN. You're not going back to that pool.

HELEN. I know...

EDWIN. We have to report this.

HELEN. I don't want any trouble, Eddie...

EDWIN. =.=

   =.=

What happened when you got out of the car?

HELEN. =.=

   =.=

> *Something did happen once* **HELEN** *got out of*
> *the car.*
> *One of the cops did grope her. But she will*
> *never give voice to it.*

> **HELEN** *walks away.* **EDWIN** *follows.*

EDWIN. Helen…

> (**JANICE**, *in the present of 1992, speaks to us.*

JANICE. Evidence.

Proof.

It is everything and

nothing.

> *Shift.*

Night. In my living room.

I go over the alumni engagement reports for the college.

The Provost wants me to focus on enticing donations from recent graduates.

(The college often receives the most contributions from women who graduated ten, twenty years ago. Men – thirty or thirty-five years ago.)

I try to explain to the Provost young people lack the empathy to give back.

Especially young men in their twenties.

She tells me I'm wrong. Her twenty-three-year-old son is the most giving person she knows.

Can that be true? Really?

I give her a binder – data, documentation that verifies my point.

She flips thru as a courtesy. Decides what she feels holds more weight than what has been studied, analyzed.

My colleague agrees with her. He says his twenty-seven year-old has grown into an empathetic wonder.

I must carve out a plan based on feeling.

I press the binder against my chest, a buoy in a river of perception.

=.=

After that Saturday with...with the police,

a silence settles in the house.

My parents and I have always been fairly quiet and calm when we're at home, but this, this silence is new.

The days carry us from that Saturday and as the next one approaches this...this weight of emptiness appears.

It is Friday evening and for the first time in over ten years, Mama and I will not go for a swim the following morning.

=.=

Saturday.

Five forty-five a.m.: I lie in my room and from my parent's bedroom at the other end of the hall, I can feel Helen's restlessness – a desperation to press against the push into...

despair? Rage?

Six a.m.: she's up. I can hear the bathroom door click shut.

Six twenty a.m.: she's downstairs. Water surges through the pipes and out the kitchen faucet.

Six thirty a.m.: the smell of brewing coffee.

Then stillness. Stillness.

I stay in my room, buried under the sheets, and wait for the clock to display the first set of p.m. numbers.

Twelve ten p.m.: I head downstairs to discover Mama at the kitchen table, reading.

> *In 1973,* **HELEN** *reads at the kitchen table.* **JANICE** *enters the moment and watches her mom read.*

> *She watches her mom, but speaks to us:*

It's a Xeroxed copy of the local police department's rule and procedure manual.

=.=

I am fifteen when I see this.

=.=

I don't ask Helen why she's reading this.

=.=

And yet I know, you know?

Years later, on my own couch in my own living room,

as I re-read the reports my provost dismissed.

=.=

...a buoy in a rushing river of perception, transgression –

> *In 1973,* **HELEN** *speaks to her fifteen-year-old daughter.*

HELEN. Hungry?

> **JANICE** *replies.*

JANICE. I just want some water.

HELEN. You should eat something.

You've been in your room all morning.

JANICE. I'll make a sandwich later.

HELEN. Later will be dinnertime, Janice.

> **JANICE** *innocently walks to glance at the page her mom reads.*
> *Curious. A pause. Confusion.* **HELEN** *looks to* **JANICE**. *The knowing settles in.*

> **JANICE** *breaks it.*

JANICE. Where's Daddy?

HELEN. Helping his brother pick out a new suit.

JANICE. Why does Uncle Dougie need a new suit?

HELEN. He's proposing to Sherri.

Their two-year anniversary is next week.

JANICE. *(To us.)* Sherri turns Uncle Dougie down.

He never wears that suit again.

(To **HELEN**.*)* That's so romantic.

They're gonna be happy together. I like Sherri.

HELEN. *(A bit of shade in 1973.)* Sherri likes Sherri, too…

JANICE. *(To us.)* On the page facing mom, I see the heading:

"Codes of Ethics"…

> **JANICE** *returns to 1992.*

> **HELEN** *remains at the kitchen table in 1973, reading.*

> **JANICE** *speaks to us.*

In my living room, I look up to see

Brendan, my oldest.

He rubs the sleepiness in his eyes.

He tells me he's thirsty.

This thirst is code.

When he has nightmares he finds me and asks for water.

He tugs at his *Tiny Toons* pajamas.

Crawls onto the couch and leans into me.

For a few moments I continue to read the reports,

until I feel his weight press – he's already asleep.

I close the binder. And hold him.

Meditate to my child's breathing.

> *It's possible* **JANICE** *closes her eyes.*
> *And does this...meditates to Brendan's breathing.*
>
> *Shift.*
>
> **HELEN** *leaves the moment.* **JANICE** *speaks to us.*

Two weeks after that...Saturday with the police,

I start to pull away from my mother...and father.

I worry the silence, the weight may stay with us forever.

But I don't know how to make it go away.

We carry ourselves from who we were

towards something else...

Helen is restless come Friday evening

> *In 1973,* **HELEN** *is indeed restless in mid-conversation with* **EDWIN**.

HELEN. Do what?

EDWIN. Dancing.

Let me take you out dancing.

HELEN. Why would we go out dancing?

EDWIN. Why would anyone go out danc–

HELEN. No, we can't leave Janice at home by herself.

EDWIN. She's fifteen.

HELEN. I don't want to leave her home by herself.

EDWIN. Why?

HELEN. I worry.

EDWIN. She'll be fine. I promise you.

    (Calls out.)

Baby girl!

JANICE. *(Calls out.)* Yes?

HELEN. Eddie…

EDWIN. *(Calls out.)* Your mama and I want to go out tonight, are you gonna be okay here by yourself?

JANICE. *(Calls out.)* Yes!

EDWIN. *(Calls out.)* Thank you!

    (To **HELEN.***)* See?

HELEN. Why this sudden urge to go out?

EDWIN. Because you feel…

HELEN. I feel…

EDWIN. Like you need to move.

Let me take you moving.

    JANICE *speaks to us.*

JANICE. I'm asleep when they get back.

They are asleep when I head out the next morning.

My lab partner in Geology II wants to start an environmental club at school.

I bike to her house for a brainstorm session.

Just as my meeting comes to an end there,

back at the house –

> *In 1973,* **GAYLE**, *in her 30s, greets a groggy and hungover* **HELEN**.

GAYLE. Heeeeeeeyyyyyy!

> *A swaying hug.*
> *The sways are too much for* **HELEN**'s *stomach.*
> *The "heeeeeeyyyyy" is too much for her headache.*

Are you surprised to see me?

HELEN. I am…

GAYLE. You should be.

I'm surprised to see me.

HELEN. When did you get in?

GAYLE. Not long ago.

I planned to call last night,

but…it looks like that call would've gone unanswered.

HELEN. Eddie and I –

GAYLE. Are getting separated?

HELEN. What? No…

GAYLE. I'm joking…

HELEN. He took me out last night.

GAYLE. He took you out?

You two still have fun?

HELEN. Gayle...

GAYLE. You want some coffee?

Let me make you some –

HELEN. Yes, I think I should probably have some.

My lord, it's noon.

You know the last time I slept in this late?

GAYLE. You missed your swim time with Janice?

HELEN. Oh, oh...no.

That's...not happening...this week.

GAYLE. Where is Janice?

HELEN. She's at a friend's house.

GAYLE. Thank goodness.

HELEN. ??

GAYLE. The girl will be sixteen in a few months,

she needs to stop being up under you and Eddie.

HELEN. She is not "up under" us.

GAYLE. Either way, it's good for her to start getting out. Where do you keep the coffee cups?

HELEN. *(Points to the cups.)* We don't keep Jance in the basement.

GAYLE. Ask <u>her</u> that...

> **GAYLE** *places a cup in front of* **HELEN** *who catches a glimpse of the wedding ring on her finger.*

> **HELEN** *stops* **GAYLE.** *Grabs the hand.*

HELEN. =.=

GAYLE. =.=

HELEN. When did this happen?

GAYLE. Three days ago.

HELEN. No invitation?

GAYLE. No one got an invitation.

We went to City Hall and –

HELEN. Here in Beacon?

GAYLE. What? No. Uh-uh.

HELEN. Why do you say it like that?

GAYLE. I would not get married in Beacon.

HELEN. Your home?

You wouldn't get married at home.

GAYLE. This is my home<u>town</u>. There's a difference...

    JANICE, *fifteen, appears.* **GAYLE** *turns to her.*

There's my little tootsie roll...!!

    Without saying a word **JANICE** *goes to*
    GAYLE *and hugs her.*
    Clings to her.
    It surprises (and hurts?) **HELEN**.
    It even surprises **GAYLE**.

HELEN. I guess she's happy to see you.

    JANICE *speaks to us.*

JANICE. Aunt Gayle floated in and out of Beacon all while
I was a kid.

But she always wrote letters,

and always included a small trinket for me.

I was the only thing that made her an aunt,

and she took the role very seriously...

Growing up, she felt like a cross breeze that glided

through a hot house.

From my late teens into my twenties,

she always seems to appear when I feel lost.

I hug her.

A stable temporary.

She smells like earth.

> *Shift.*

> *Everyone, post-dinner, that night.*
> *'70s soul music plays from the player.**

GAYLE, JANICE, HELEN, EDWIN.

GAYLE*'s new husband, Bobby, is there too.*
But his presence is implied.
We shouldn't need to see another body...

JANICE *is enthralled by* **GAYLE.**

GAYLE. ...and when I say knocked out, I mean I was in a deep sleep.

That float-with-the-ancestors type sleep.

I could've missed my chance, that phonecall altogether.

But you know those times when you're

heavy in a dream world and a noise in the real

world makes its way to you?

---

* A license to produce THE RIPPLE, THE WAVE THAT CARRIED ME HOME does not include a performance license for any third-party or copyrighted music. Licensees should create an original composition or use music in the public domain. For further information, please see the Music and Third-Party Materials Use Note on page iii.

My telephone came to me.

Floated to me.

I was in a field hunting with Granddaddy and –

HELEN. What?

GAYLE. That's the dream I was having:

I was hunting wild turkey with Granddaddy.

HELEN. When did you ever hunt with Granddaddy?

GAYLE. It was a dream, Helen.

I never said I…

> **GAYLE** *giggles with* **JANICE**.

HELEN. I know what a dream is…

EDWIN. *(Mediating?)* So the telephone floated to you
and…

> **EDWIN** *pecks* **HELEN** *on the check. Or some
> other reassuring gesture.* **HELEN** *eases.*

GAYLE. And the next thing I know

I'm awake, receiver in hand and professor's voice says:

"So-and-so can't come with us to the dig in Martinique.
Can you meet us at the airport in an hour?"

> **JANICE** *speaks to us.*

JANICE. Gayle spent a month working

on an archeological dig.

Sifting, gathering, tagging.

Discoveries in the sunlight.

Quiet meals at dusk.

Dreams in pure moonlight.

This is where she met Bobby.

He is gorgeous.

He sits next to me at the dinner table.

He smells like Gayle.

Soil and dry foliage and...

I am fifteen and they are the greatest couple I know.

> *Shift.*
> **GAYLE** *and* **JANICE** *are alone.*
>
> **GAYLE** *reveals a necklace with a small pendant filled with soil.*

Did you bring that back from Martinique...?

> **GAYLE** *nods.*

GAYLE. Don't tell your mom.

She'll come up with some reason

to make it dangerous and take it away.

> **JANICE** *slips on the necklace.*
> *Shifts the soil from side to side.*
>
> **GAYLE** *exits.*

JANICE. *(To us.)* I am seventeen.

And I want nothing to do with tanks, chlorine, H_2O.

It is the spring of 1975.

I have not touched a body of water in two years.

In school I'm obsessed with earth sciences – specifically geology and agriculture. Water is necessary for evolution, vegetation, but it is no longer my politics, my cause.

At this point Edwin and Helen have spent my entire life, trying to reopen Brookside.

They worked on campaign staffs for candidates who promised pool access.

They petitioned an investigation into the city's funding allocation.

Edwin even tried running for city controller...

All the while Brookside remained closed, abandoned.

Indoor pool clubs are wildly popular in Beacon.

All of them privately owned and operated.

And each one has its own tier of exclusivity.

All of these clubs are willing to pay Black folks to launder towels, serve refreshments, mop the decks.

But none of them are interested in accepting the fees or applications from Blacks to become members.

Edwin (of course) submits an application to each club, and is denied by each club.

His demand for access appeared revolutionary in the 1960s, but now looks desperate in the '70s.

There is now a rising generation of Black folks who have no direct memory of Brookside.

Swimming has become a "white thing."

And it embarrasses me to hear people question Edwin's motives, diagnose his thinking.

His determination (obsession?) clashes against the Afrocentric attitudes among the young Necessity and Thinking Blacks.

=.=

With his stockpile of rejected, yet flawless, applications, Daddy convinces a lawyer to represent his discrimination lawsuit against the pool clubs.

My disinterest, disgust is palpable.

=.=

Aunt Gayle and Uncle Bobby bought a small farm in Tennessee.

I write her a letter, ask to visit this summer.

She writes back: yes.

> **JANICE** *is seventeen.* **EDWIN** *is with her. Mid-conversation:*

EDWIN. Go down to that farm? For what?

JANICE. To help them.

EDWIN. With what?

JANICE. Whatever they need help with, Daddy.

EDWIN. You think working a farm, dawn to dusk

  is anything like the projects you do at school?

JANICE. I know it'll be hard work.

  It'll be different from school.

  It'll be real life and I want to do it. I can work hard.

EDWIN. I know you're a hard worker, Janice.

  Nobody could say otherwise.

JANICE. So I can go?

EDWIN. What about the trial?

  It'd be so good to have you in the gallery,

  seated next to your mother.

> **JANICE** *is a bit hesitant.*
> *This is the first time she's ever contradicted her father.*

JANICE. I don't want to go to the trial.

       HELEN *enters the scene.*

EDWIN. *(To* **HELEN**.*)* Do you hear your daughter?

(To **JANICE**.*)* How could you not want to be a part of this?

My discrimination lawsuit against these pool clubs is finally getting its day in court.

We've been fighting for so long.

This case going to trial is the first real win we've had in years.

JANICE. *(Still uneasy.)* It…it isn't my fight, Daddy.

       Courage is a bit stronger.

The land is a part of who we are too, Daddy.

EDWIN. Excuse me?

JANICE. Uncle Dougie told me stories about your side of the family.

How they were farmers down south before they migrated here to Kansas.

Working with the land is a part of you, which means it's a part of me.

EDWIN. You're trying to tell <u>me</u> about my own history?

JANICE. No, I just…

I want to hold something, work with something real!

Aunt Gayle and her husband <u>own</u> that land.

EDWIN. Being in debt is not ownership.

JANICE. You don't know if they're in debt.

EDWIN. And you do?

JANICE. I know it's work.

Being there, on that land, is real work.

I want to work.

I feel like this family's been dancing with an impossibility my entire life.

Water literally slips between our fingers.

White folks fight to keep us from it.

Why do I need it?

Why should I want it?

HELEN. Stop, Janice.

JANICE. Why?

HELEN. Because your mouth is running faster than your head and –

JANICE. And what?

I might speak the truth?

I don't want to spend my life chasing after white people

begging them to let me play with their toys.

What has this fight gotten us?

Point to one good thing that's happened for the three of us?

Both of you fight these battles against white folks

who don't want anything to do with you.

Why can't you two face the fact that you will never win?

> **EDWIN** *raises his hand to strike* **JANICE.** *Freezes mid-swing.*

> **JANICE** *speaks to us:*

I hadn't been hit since that fight in third grade.

> **JANICE** *collapses to the ground.*

This hit is unlike any physical pain I had known.

It shook everything, all of me.

My daddy's force.

Jesus. The air yanked from my body.

Lungs, once so strong and controlled in the water,

fall weak at the strike of my daddy's hand.

Mama grabs at him.

I fall to the carpet.

It's a cartoon – stars, my ears ringing.

It is real. I'm on the floor. My head spinning.

> **EDWIN** *and* **HELEN** *exit the moment.* **JANICE** *is left alone.*
>
> *In 1992 the cordless phone rings.*
>
> **JANICE** *answers it (a bit groggy).*

Hello...?

> *Note: although their exchange is a phone call,* **YOUNG CHIPPER AMBITIOUS BLACK WOMAN** *should be present onstage during this scene.*

YOUNG CHIPPER AMBITIOUS BLACK WOMAN. Hi Mrs. Clifton!

This is Young Chipper Ambitious Black Woman...

JANICE. Oh! Yes. Hello. Hi.

YOUNG CHIPPER AMBITIOUS BLACK WOMAN. Did I wake you?

JANICE. No, no.

YOUNG CHIPPER AMBITIOUS BLACK WOMAN. I know it's late in the evening, but it's been a week since we last spoke. And I promised I'd call you once the time had passed.

I was just about to leave the office, then I remembered: call Mrs. Clifton!

JANICE. Mm-hm.

YOUNG CHIPPER AMBITIOUS BLACK WOMAN. Were you able to give more thought to our invitation?

JANICE. What do you do, Chipper?

YOUNG CHIPPER AMBITIOUS BLACK WOMAN. Pardon?

JANICE. You were about to leave the office.

Does the Af-Am Recognition Committee have its own office?

YOUNG CHIPPER AMBITIOUS BLACK WOMAN. Oh. Well. No.

My work with the committee is primarily voluntary.

JANICE. So the office you were about to leave…?

YOUNG CHIPPER AMBITIOUS BLACK WOMAN. Oh. I'm an assistant at a local marketing company.

JANICE. Do you like that work?

YOUNG CHIPPER AMBITIOUS BLACK WOMAN. Well, the team is really smart and passionate.

And I've learned so much in the short time I've been here.

JANICE. Are you the only one?

YOUNG CHIPPER AMBITIOUS BLACK WOMAN. =.=

What do you mean?

JANICE. You know what I mean.

> **YOUNG CHIPPER AMBITIOUS BLACK WOMAN** *does, indeed know what* **JANICE** *means.*

YOUNG CHIPPER AMBITIOUS BLACK WOMAN. =.=

=.=

Yes.

JANICE. And how has that been?

> *It's possible* **YOUNG CHIPPER AMBITIOUS BLACK WOMAN** *gets real in this next section. As real as she can get. Which may not be as real as other folks, but it's pretty damn real for Young Chipper Ambitious Black Woman.*

YOUNG CHIPPER AMBITIOUS BLACK WOMAN. As good as it can be for any Black woman who is the only anything or everything.

=.=

Are you the only one?

At your office?

JANICE. In my office?

No.

But I am the only one who is a director of anything.

So. There are several meetings in a week when I am the only one.

> **JANICE** *and* **YOUNG CHIPPER AMBITIOUS BLACK WOMAN** *sigh a knowing, understanding sigh.*

What generation Beacon are you?

YOUNG CHIPPER AMBITIOUS BLACK WOMAN. Second.

JANICE. You plan on staying.

YOUNG CHIPPER AMBITIOUS BLACK WOMAN. I do.

I'll probably go to a state school for my masters,

but I'll definitely return.

JANICE. *(Genuine.)* Why?

YOUNG CHIPPER AMBITIOUS BLACK WOMAN. It's my home.

JANICE. Have you always seen Beacon that way?

As your home?

YOUNG CHIPPER AMBITIOUS BLACK WOMAN. Yes. Well…

=.=

If I'm truly honest…

not until I joined the Af-Am Recognition Committee.

Before that Beacon felt like a place I grew up in.

A place that held the people I care about.

JANICE. What happened when you joined?

YOUNG CHIPPER AMBITIOUS BLACK WOMAN. It helped me feel the "home" in my hometown.

I realized there has to be an exchange of positive impact

to feel like I belong here.

This place affected me. In many ways it shaped who I am, but I also feel like I'm shaping it.

I want my city to recognize my people's contribution.

And I want to celebrate that in an open, public way.

(Joking…) And now I feel like I'm rambling…

I promise you, Mrs. Clifton, I did not intend to turn this conversation into a stump speech.

> *Light laughter from* **YOUNG CHIPPER AMBITIOUS BLACK WOMAN.** *Unbeknownst to her, her words resonate deeply with* **JANICE.**

JANICE. It isn't a ramble, Chipper. You, you make a lot of sense...

=.=

And call me Janice.

=.=

I'll be there.

At the naming ceremony.

YOUNG CHIPPER AMBITIOUS BLACK WOMAN. You will?

JANICE. Yes.

YOUNG CHIPPER AMBITIOUS BLACK WOMAN. And you'll say a few words, Janice?

JANICE. Yes.

> *Shift. 1975.*
> **JANICE** *slips on a pair of large shades to cover the bruise on her face.*
> *Greyhound bus sounds.*
> *We travel from Kansas to Tennessee.* **JANICE** *speaks to us:*

Mama and Daddy send me to Tennessee.

> **JANICE,** *seventeen, sits in Aunt Gayle's kitchen in Tennessee.*

> **AUNT GAYLE** *is in her mid-30s.* **JANICE** *slowly removes her shades.*

Note: The appearance of the bruise can be implied by Gayle's reaction. We shouldn't need any makeup on Janice's face.

AUNT GAYLE *lets out an audible wince when she gets a full-on view of the damage.*

AUNT GAYLE. Dayyyyyyum. Janice...

Janice...

What the hell did you say to that man...?

JANICE. This bruise is the only reason I'm here.

AUNT GAYLE. ??

JANICE. The local news is following Daddy's trial.

They don't want their daughter's face published in the papers.

AUNT GAYLE. Oooooo,

(À la James Brown.) "Papa don't take no mess..."

JANICE *smiles. It hurts to smile.*

She winces.

JANICE. You can't be your entertaining self, Aunt Gayle.

Not until this gets a bit less tender.

AUNT GAYLE. You put anything on it?

JANICE. Nothing but a cold compress the night it happened.

AUNT GAYLE *retrieves a small unlabeled jar.*

AUNT GAYLE. Let's put some aloe on it.

It'll help reduce irritation.

AUNT GAYLE *is careful, gentle applying the gel. It smarts, but **JANICE** stays cool.*

JANICE. It looks awful, doesn't it?

AUNT GAYLE. It'll heal up.

Until then…it's not so pretty,

but it'll heal.

=.=

You know…

me and my daddy clashed.

Right before I left Beacon.

JANICE. What happened with Granddaddy?

AUNT GAYLE. He kept trying to give me his idea of freedom,

but I wanted to earn my own.

JANICE. Mhm.

Did you fix things?

AUNT GAYLE. He tried…

I tried…

=.=

You'll have to learn how to face your daddy again, Janice.

Or at least try…

JANICE. =.=

=.=

I hate that I feel embarrassed.

=.=

For the entire trip I had my head held

down, these dark shades on…

when it wasn't even my fault.

AUNT GAYLE. =.=

JANICE. Why doesn't he get to be ashamed?

AUNT GAYLE. Who said he isn't?

JANICE. I do. Me.

AUNT GAYLE. Did he apologize?

JANICE. After the swelling.

   When this patch of dark purple

   and blue started showing...

   =.=

   The act didn't seem to shock him

   but the evidence of it did.

AUNT GAYLE. Well... I know you start

   college in the fall, but

   you can stay here as long as

   you want this summer.

   Just doesn't have to be the six weeks.

JANICE. Thank you...

> **JANICE** *speaks to us in the present of 1992,*
> *but it's possible she doesn't shift her position*
> *from* **AUNT GAYLE.**

(To us.) I remember Aunt Gayle looks so beautiful on
the farm.

I mean, I always thought she was beautiful.

But she is so breathtaking in that nature.

   =.=

   =.=

I accept her invitation to stay for the entire summer.

=.=

Working on the farm with her and Uncle Bobby

are some of the best months of my life.

    AUNT GAYLE *exits.*

I return to Beacon with only a few weeks to pack for college.

Daddy tries to acknowledge how we left things before my time on the farm, but I'm too angry (ashamed?) to really participate.

My parents and I are cordial, but distant.

    EDWIN *and* **HELEN** *appear.*
    JANICE *continues to speak to us, as they hug and kiss their daughter goodbye on the day they drop her off at college.*
    It's possible **EDWIN** *discreetly wipes away a tear.*

    EDWIN *and* **HELEN** *exit.*

While I'm away at school, I call the house often.

Around this time the Sunday Polites begin.

The three of us speak to each other, but never really have conversations.

I can't help but feel the countless times they chose the movement, not me.

The years are panes of glass that accumulate between us.

I can see them, and they see me, but our language is forever filtered.

Even at Daddy's funeral, quietly reeling from the sudden shock of the loss,

I can't look my mother in the eye for more than a moment.

I'm ashamed by this and keep mostly to myself during the service,

not knowing how to be with Helen without Edwin.

Shift.

1992.

I will go alone.

To Beacon.

For the naming ceremony.

=.=

I am nervous about this trip to my hometown.

But nostalgic for the ways it felt...could still feel like home. The night before I leave,

I sit in my living room.

My boys, my husband – all asleep.

I sit on the couch with photos

and other keepsakes from my childhood.

=.=

And then...then I discover the letters my mother wrote to me during my summer in Tennessee. She's careful not to talk too much about the trial.

Spares many details about my father...

> **HELEN,** *in her 40s, 1975.*
> *Recites excerpts from the letters.*

HELEN. ...the lawyer is optimistic.

...I've been at the courthouse every day.

...your father and I were up late last night to prep for his appearance on the stand.

JANICE. In my replies, I don't mention how free I feel at the farm.

Uncle Bobby is fluent in French.

He teaches me French as we work the farm.

I speak a romance language to the land.

It is not long before I am in love with this land.

I confess this to Aunt Gayle, not Mama.

=.=

As I sit in my living room, I read Helen's letters in order

and notice a gradual shift... the slow opening

of reflection; consideration...

HELEN. *(From the letter.)* ...I sit in the courtroom and sometimes...

sometimes I'm in awe...other times I'm so

disappointed...and yet at times I'm furious...

but I remain still, my face neutral as I sit

in that courtroom.

I wonder how did I end up seated in the gallery.

Not in the literal sense, of course, but...

but how did the events in my life lead me to

a trial?

=.=

I had dreams for Brookside when I was your age.

I wanted to start an all Black swim team at my high school,

my daddy would be the head coach

and I would be the captain.

(a position I'd earn, of course)

We'd win local and national competitions.

When I return to Beacon after college,

I'd take over as head coach when Daddy retires.

In my life plan, right now, it'd be my fifteenth season as swim coach.

In my plan, I'd give you the gift of knowing water's power and peace...

=.=

...I am so disappointed in my hometown, my own country.

The simplicity of my desires...

it breaks my heart to sit in that courtroom...

to have to fight for the simplicity of freedom...

of joy...

JANICE. In my living room, my family asleep,

I sit on the couch in tears.

I'm in Ohio. A grown woman's years in my hands –

Helen's years

my own years reflected...

=.=

I do not remember reading this when I was seventeen.

Or was I too young to really see these words?

Understand her vulnerability?

As I read these moments from my mother's life now

I realize why I question

all the weight given to my father's memory.

I've seen the hushed sacrifices my mother has made.

Felt those choices whether I understood them or not.

When I look back, I realize she was infinitely stronger
than me – in and out of the water.

=.=

=.=

I read her letters again and again.

And try to recall my replies from Tennessee…

> *In 1975* **HELEN** *opens a letter from* **JANICE**.
> *Reads it aloud:*

HELEN. "Dear mother:

It has gotten hot here as we're in the peak of summer,
Aunt Gayle says.

It hasn't rained since I've been here.

And while the land is far from drought;

it is definitely parched.

I asked Uncle Bobby how to say 'we hope for water'

It is: 'nous espérons de l'eau' …"

> **JANICE** *steps out of the moment. We're fully
> in 1975.*
> **HELEN** *has just finished reading Janice's
> letter.*
> **EDWIN** *enters loosening his tie from another
> day at trial.*

EDWIN. How is she?

HELEN. Good.

She's happy.

EDWIN. Happy is good.

HELEN. You should write her.

EDWIN. I know...

HELEN. Or send her something.

EDWIN. I'll call down there this weekend.

> **HELEN** *returns the letter to the envelope.*

HELEN. Call this weekend. Write a letter tonight.

EDWIN. I know...

HELEN. Do you?

EDWIN. Can we please...

Just relax for a few moments...?

It's been a long day...

HELEN. =.=

EDWIN. Please...?

HELEN. =.=

EDWIN. I wish you were sitting next to me.

During the trial.

I wish I could hold your hand.

Feel the comfort of these hands.

HELEN. I'd prefer if you sat next <u>to me</u>.

Then neither one of us would be the plaintiff in this discrimination lawsuit.

EDWIN. Who, if not us?

HELEN. I do wish I could hold your hand.

I do.

Your brother isn't easy to sit next to.

So anxious. He watches the proceedings like it's a boxing match in a library.

Mimics Dougie's muted gesture, movements.

I remind him people are looking.

He pats me on the knee –

Stiff pat on **EDWIN**'s *knee.*

like I'm a newlywed wife who doesn't

understand the ins and outs of the sport.

EDWIN. He means well.

=.=

=.=

Our lawyer wants to meet with us before tomorrow's session.

HELEN. About what?

EDWIN. My guess?

To prepare us for defeat.

=.=

Do you feel like we could lose this?

HELEN. Honestly... I don't know.

EDWIN. =.=

Me neither.

=.=

I think we have a solid case, but...

HELEN. The other side paints

every piece of our evidence

as if it's an opinion.

EDWIN. Exactly.

HELEN. =.=

=.=

Babe...

come the end of this trial

win or lose

let's not fight anymore.

EDWIN. Are we fighting?

HELEN. Not me and you...

Us and these white folks in Beacon.

Me and you against these social institutions...

You and your daughter –

EDWIN. I will make things right with her.

HELEN. When?

EDWIN. I can't do it with just a letter, a phone call.

HELEN. You can <u>start it</u> with a letter, or a phone call...

EDWIN. If we win this case, we won't have to fight any more.

It'll be a huge victory for every Black person in Beacon...

HELEN. We can't win the game they designed, Eddie.

As soon as we catch up, the rules change...

EDWIN. You're giving up on our dream?

HELEN. I'm finding new dreams...

Reworking the old ones...

=.=

=.=

There's a chance we can reopen Brookside.

EDWIN. What? How?

HELEN. I had lunch with Brenda Sparks.

The Public Works Board approached her brother about filling an upcoming vacancy.

EDWIN. They're putting a brotha on that board?

HELEN. Yes. It hasn't been announced yet but it is happening.

EDWIN. Love, one man can't reopen Brookside.

HELEN. But <u>two</u> men can set the wheels in motion.

EDWIN. ??

HELEN. This can finally be our chance to lease Brookside from the city.

EDWIN. But we tried that before –

HELEN. I know but consider what's different this time.

Now we have Brenda's brother.

You can work with him to draft the terms.

EDWIN. *(Catching on.)* And my lawyer got us access to the private pool leasing agreements…

HELEN. Yes.

Now we know the preferential terms the city made for all the white pool owners.

EDWIN. And those terms can be <u>our</u> anchor.

HELEN. Exactly.

You can make this happen.

EDWIN. =.=

HELEN. Brookside can be a privately managed space that we can decide how it's cared for.

We can jumpstart renovations with the money Daddy
left us.

And gift the pool to the community.

=.=

I think we can do it, Eddie.

EDWIN. It'll take some time...

=.=

But this change could drum up fresh support...

we can get the church behind it.

HELEN. And all the allies you've made during this trial...

EDWIN. ...we can finally restart your daddy's swim program...

make it free for everyone in the community.

...start a partnership with the public schools...

> *Dreaming.*

...maybe...finally build a community center...raise

the money to build an indoor pool so we can swim all

year-round...

> *A moment as* **EDWIN** *silently weighs the*
> *possibility...*
> *It could work. He smiles.*
> *Hugs* **HELEN**.
> *A kiss.*

> *The moment with* **HELEN** *and* **EDWIN** *ends.*
> *In 1992, airport sounds in Ohio.*

> **JANICE** *stands with her purse and small*
> *carry-on.*

> *In shock.*

She looks up at the fourth wall where the airport TV plays news footage about the Rodney King verdict.

From the TV we hear:

REPORTER. Two jurors talked to ABC news today by phone...

JUROR. Everybody's saying,

"this videotape, this videotape"...

=.=

But...

these officers have...a job to do.

And doing that job

they have to be given a certain amount of reasonable –

see, and that's what this is...you know, reasonable force.

> **JANICE** *speaks to us.*

JANICE. Not guilty.

=.=

I am the only Black woman at the terminal.

I'm flying from Ohio to Kansas.

> *Audio from news reports*...

REPORTER. The jurors felt it was King who controlled the action.

That he could've stopped the beating by surrendering.

---

*A license to produce THE RIPPLE, THE WAVE THAT CARRIED ME HOME does not include a performance license for any third-party or copyrighted recordings or images. Licensees must acquire rights for any copyrighted recordings or images or create their own.

Sounds of a plane taking flight.

JANICE. I am the only one on the flight.

Stunned, but knowing, understanding it was inevitable.

"Reasonable force…"

One hundred and nine minutes later, wheels touch down in Kansas.

Sounds of wheels touching down.

I am the last one off the plane.

The last one to leave the terminal.

The first thing I see is a sign with my name.

A bright, heart-shaped brown face framed by a sea

of dark hair.

It's Young Chipper Ambitious Black Woman who holds the sign.

She's volunteered to pick me up from the airport.

She is the first Black face I see following the acquittal.

We hug. Like strangers, like family, like sisters, like aliens traumatized by our time on this dysfunctional planet.

1992, Beacon, Kansas.

JANICE *sits with* **AUNT GAYLE** *and* **HELEN.**
*They watch the LA riots on television.**

At some point during the conversation, we notice **HELEN** *moves a bit slowly.*

---

* A license to produce THE RIPPLE, THE WAVE THAT CARRIED ME HOME does not include a performance license for any third-party or copyrighted recordings or images. Licensees must acquire rights for any copyrighted recordings or images or create their own.

She is in the early stages of Parkinson's.

(From the TV:)

REPORTER. All central streets leading into the

area are now closed…as night falls

this aerial view shows us the streets

are ablaze…

AUNT GAYLE. They're trying to keep them

contained – that's why the roads are closed.

Let them burn their own streets.

If I planned that riot, right before

the verdict was announced,

we would've caravanned to Rodeo Drive and Beverly
Hills…

HELEN. Listen to you…

riots don't have a coordinator.

That's not how they work –

AUNT GAYLE. Well maybe they should we'd be better off
for it.

You think they'll cancel the naming ceremony?

JANICE. Young Chipper thinks the event can bring the
community together.

HELEN. Can you imagine if something like that happened
here?

AUNT GAYLE. It did – those white mobs back when we
were kids…

HELEN. That's not the same.

AUNT GAYLE. Why not?

HELEN. A mob is not a riot, Gayle.

AUNT GAYLE. The only difference is they were beating Black folks instead of storefronts.

Pssshhh, when they first integrated Gregory Lane.

HELEN. Please, don't talk about that again…

(*To* **JANICE**.) She's been telling pool stories ever since they announced the name change.

AUNT GAYLE. 1957: a hundred young white men with sticks, chains, ropes, and bricks swinging at any brown head they saw.

We were all Rodney King that day.

Even little kids – they didn't care.

> **HELEN** *prepares tea and some hospitable snacks.*

JANICE. Mama, let me do that…

HELEN. Sit. Sit. Sit. I'm fine.

AUNT GAYLE. (*To* **JANICE**.) Let her move.

Let her move.

It's good for her.

> **HELEN** *and* **AUNT GAYLE** *watch the TV.*

(*To* **HELEN**.) We still going to the next class?

HELEN. Yes, ma'am.

JANICE. What class?

HELEN. I joined aquatic aerobics at the community center.

It helps…with the Parkinson's and all…

AUNT GAYLE. The music is pretty good.

HELEN. A nice young Black girl teaches the class. She plays music with a nice beat.

JANICE. What time is it at?

AUNT GAYLE. Six a.m.

We go three times a week. Lord help us.

HELEN. Next time we're there, it'll have my husband's name over the doorway.

AUNT GAYLE. Won't that be something?

You should come with us, Janice.

When's the last time we were all in the water together?

It's been a long, long time…too long.

JANICE. I've been thinking a lot about that…

HELEN. *(To* **JANICE.***)* Only if you feel up to it…

No pressure…

AUNT GAYLE. Not from her maybe, but plenty from me.

> **AUNT GAYLE** *looks to the TV. Audio fades in.*

CITIZEN. I think the rioting is stupid

I think it's ridiculous

and I think people have,

probably it's,

too much democracy

too much freedom

and the people don't know what to do with it…

> **JANICE** *speaks to us.*

JANICE. We sit in front of the TV

late into the night

silenced by the footage

that conjures our own memories

of violence, destruction, hate.

Somehow

in that night

we also find humor, comfort

in sharing this time with each other.

The TV stays on through the night

into the following afternoon

until we dress for the ceremony.

Aunt Gayle tapes CNN while we're away.

It is a lovely and warm event.

Filled with people I haven't seen since Daddy's funeral.

It's...nice to come together in happier times.

Just before I go to the podium to speak,

Mama hugs me, whispers in my ear:

HELEN. Thank you.

> **JANICE** *approaches a microphone. Addresses the audience as the attendees at the ceremony.*

JANICE. I'll say only a few words.

=.=

I thank Young Chipper and the African American Recognition Committee.

I thank everyone in Beacon who made this possible.

My father was a charismatic, intelligent, passionate man.

He was also stubborn and determined.

But he never fought these fights to seek praise or fame.

He always fought for the people he cared about: all of you, all of us

in Beacon.

My father would've been humbled by this ceremony.

He would've been speechless, which would've been a first.

The only words he'd probably be able to gather would be...

to thank my mother: Helen Collen.

I'd like to read a section of a letter my mother sent me

in the summer of 1975:

"In my life plan...

I'd give you the gift of knowing water's power and peace. The joy of it.

I'd teach you how it establishes a rhythm in your life

that can sustain you for the rest of your days.

This is the gift I want for all Black people..."

> *The stage fills with blue light, resembling pool water...or maybe actual water fills the stage.*
>
> **JANICE** *steps away from the microphone.*
>
> *We sit in a meditative peace as we listen to the echo of the water lapping against the tank.*
>
> *We are in the indoor swimming facility now known as the Edwin P. Collen, Jr. pool.*
>
> *We hear footsteps against the deck. Hushed voices.*

The sound of bodies slowly submerging into the pool.

It is the six a.m. aquatic aerobics class.

HELEN *and* **GAYLE** *appear in their bathing suits.*

JANICE *appears in her bathing suit.*

(To us.) The next morning at aquatic aerobics, the instructor asks us to tap into our healing energy and we dedicate that energy to the people in LA.

The people in our home state.

The people in this entire country.

JANICE, HELEN *and* **AUNT GAYLE** *take a moment to send healing energy to themselves each other every person in the theater in the city the state the country.*

Suddenly, the instrumental version of a song in the style of "Everything's Gonna Be Alright" by Naughty by Nature plays.[*]

JANICE, *along with her mother* **HELEN** *and* **AUNT GAYLE,** *execute a series of aerobic moves while in the water.*

---

[*] A license to produce THE RIPPLE, THE WAVE THAT CARRIED ME HOME does not include a performance license for "Everything's Gonna Be Alright." The publisher and author suggest that the licensee contact ASCAP or BMI to ascertain the music publisher and contact such music publisher to license or acquire permission for performance of the song. If a license or permission is unattainable for "Everything's Gonna Be Alright," the licensee may not use the song in THE RIPPLE, THE WAVE THAT CARRIED ME HOME but should create an original composition in a similar style or use a similar song in the public domain. For further information, please see the Music and Third-Party Materials Use Note on page iii.

*There's a gradual joy and freedom as **JANICE**, **HELEN** and **AUNT GAYLE** dance in unison.*

This goes on for a while until eventually lights fade to black.

End of Play

TIMELINE OF EVENTS

(For reference.)

Playing with time a bit here...
– Following this reference timeline, Helen & Gayle are in their 50s in 1992...but following an artistic license timeline Helen & Gayle will be in their 60s.

1935
Helen is born.

1936
Edwin is born.

1939
Gayle is born.

1940
Gregory Lane opens.
SunRay opens.

1943
Brookside opens.
Janice's grandfather starts the swim program.
All three pools are segregated.

1944
Edwin is eight years old when he takes swim lessons at Brookside.

1949
Helen at fourteen starts giving swim lessons at Brookside.

1953
Helen at eighteen gives swim lessons to the two Black boys who will drown.
Edwin at seventeen/eighteen executes his SunRay pool takeover.

1956
Beacon Three drowning on March 3rd.
Funerals a week later.
Edwin and Helen start the fight to integrate pools.

1957
Judge rules all city pools integrated.
Beacon Three Remembrance begins.

1958
All city pools shut down.
The Brookside swim program ends.
Janice is born.

Early 1960s
Janice takes lessons as a toddler at Mr. Facilities' pool.

1966
Janice is eight and gets in a fight.
Janice speaks at the BT remembrance for the first time at eight.

1969
Janice is eleven when we see her play the family word game.

1973
Janice is fifteen and stops speaking at BT Remembrance.
Janice is fifteen and Helen is thirty-eight when the pullover by the police happens.
Gayle is thirty-four and marries Bobby.

1975
Edwin begins the lawsuit.
Janice is seventeen and asks to go to Tennessee to visit Gayle and Bobby.
Edwin hits Janice.
Janice goes to Tennessee.
Gayle is thirty-six.
Janice leaves for college
Helen is forty when she writes Janice letters.

1979
Brookside is reopened on April 30th.

1988
Edwin dies suddenly from a heart attack.

1992
Young Chipper reaches out to Janice.
The Rodney King trial is televised.
The Rodney King verdict is announced.
Janice returns home to Beacon.
April 30 – Janice speaks at the naming ceremony.

Rodney King real-world notes:
March 3, 1991 – the day Rodney King is beaten by the LAPD (same day in the play in 1951 when the Beacon Three drown).
April 29, 1992 – not-guilty verdict is announced and rioting begins (this is the day Janice flies back to Beacon).
May 9th, 1992 – federal troops stand down in Los Angeles (some national guards are still there as late as May 27).